The Golden Winged Fairy

The Golden Winged Fairy

written by

Lala Fae

illustrated by

Laura Siadak

madebyfae

Published in the United States by madebyfae.
Printed in China through Bolton Associates, Inc. San Rafael, CA
www.madebyfae.com

Fae, Lala.
The golden winged fairy / written by Lala Fae;
illustrated by Laura Siadak. --First edition
pages cm

SUMMARY: A fairy with one silver wing and one golden wing learns to
celebrate her difference after the glow of her golden wing guides
the silver-winged fairies safely through a dark night storm.

ISBN 978-0-9908527-3-5

1. Fairies--Juvenile fiction. 2. Individual
differences--Juvenile fiction. 3. Self-esteem--Juvenile
fiction. [1. Fairies--Fiction. 2. Individual
differences--Fiction. 3. Self-esteem--Fiction.]
I. Siadak, Laura, illustrator. II. Title.

PZ8.F163Gol 2015 [E] QBI15-600053

For Evi

&

for young fairies

Long ago, in the Land of the Silver Moon Fairies, there lived a young fairy named Lorelei.

Lorelei was no ordinary fairy, for she had two different colored wings. One wing shone silver like the wings of all Silver Moon Fairies. The other wing glowed golden as Midsummer's Day.

When the Silver Moon Fairies gathered moonbeams at midnight, Lorelei hid within.

And when the Silver Moon Fairies gathered stardust by starlight, Lorelei never joined in.

Lorelei felt ashamed of her difference and did not want her golden wing to be seen.

"You are fortunate to be different," said Lorelei's mother. But Lorelei did not agree.

More than anything she wanted to dance with the Silver Moon Fairies. More than anything she wanted to be just like them. So . . .

. . . on Midsummer's Night when the moon shone bright, and the Silver Moon Fairies danced, Lorelei held a handful of fairy dust and . . .

. . . sprinkled her golden wing.

Silver-winged, now, like all Silver Moon Fairies, Lorelei joined in the dance, circling round and round with the Silver Moon Fairies as midsummer's moon rose high.

But then, without warning . . .

. . . the midnight moon darkened, as storm clouds filled the sky. And raindrops washed fairy dust from Lorelei's wing as a golden glow lit the night.

Frightened and fast, her wing now aglow, Lorelei flew all the way home.

With early morn came a knock at the door, the Silver Moon Fairies outside. "The glow of your golden wing guided us home. You saved us from the storm!"

From that day ever after, Lorelei danced by the light of the moon with the Silver Moon Fairies deep in the forest, one wing silver and the other wing, glowing golden true.

May you
always
glow golden

This story has been transcribed by Lala Fae from ancient fairy archives with deepest reverence for the fairy elders, keepers and protectors of fairy lore, and heartfelt gratitude to young fairies of all ages and lands, the stewards and conservators of our natural world.